Hound Dawg

Patricia Vermillion

illustrations by Cheryl Pilgrim

TCU Press
Fort Worth, TX

Library of Congress Cataloging-in-Publication Data

Vermillion, Patricia, author.
 Hound Dawg / by Patricia Vermillion ; illustrated by Cheryl Pilgrim.
    pages cm
 Summary: "Hound Dawg is a southern-style retelling of "The Little Red
Hen," in which the lazy Hound Dawg refuses to help the other barn-
yard animals raise a corn plant, grind the corn, and then make
cornbread. It is only when thieving Raccoon goes after the
cornbread that Hound Dawg finally proves his worth and
chases Raccoon away, thereby earning his fair share
of the cornbread" Provided by publisher.
 Includes bibliographical references.
 ISBN 978-0-87565-615-1 (alk. paper)
[1. Folklore.] I. Pilgrim, Cheryl, illustrator. II. Title.
 PZ8.1.V4775Ho 2015
 398.2--dc23

                         2015021467

Text design by Rebecca A. Allen

TCU Press
TCU Box 298300
Fort Worth, TX 76109
817.257.7822
www.prs.tcu.edu

To order books call 1.800.826.8911

To all of my friends at the
Lamplighter School

Way back in the day, Hound Dawg lived on a cotton farm with Bessie, Calico, and Penny.

Ah-WOOOOOOOOOO

But Hound Dawg? Why he never worked a lick. The only thing he did was bark and howl.

One blistering morning, Hound Dawg spotted something new growing out of his dirt patch by the front porch.

Too lazy to look for himself
he yawned, "Who'll see what's
sprouting over yonder?"

"Bless my butter," Bessie said. "I'll do it. . . . Well, if that don't beat all. It's a cornstalk."

Hound Dawg licked his lips. "A cornstalk? Makes me hungry for some good ol' southern cornbread. Who's gonna water that stalk so it'll grow?"

"Great balls of fur," Calico said. "I'll do it."

Every day that stalk grew bigger . . . and bigger . . . and bigger.

"Now, who's gonna pluck that corn off the cob?" Calico asked.

"Well, scramble my eggs. I'll do it," Penny said. "But if I do the plucking, who's gonna mix and bake the cornbread?"

"Don't look at me . . .
I don't know nothing about
making cornbread." Hound
Dawg woofed once and fell
fast asleep.

"Looks like Hound Dawg won't be helping a-tall," Bessie bellowed angrily. Calico hissed. Penny cackled.

So they worked together without him.

Bessie added her buttermilk,

Calico raked in the corn,

and Penny cracked in her eggs and mixed it all up.

Finally, hauling his bones up off the porch, Hound Dawg hollered, "I'm starving for some good ol' southern cornbread."

"Ain't that so," Calico hissed.
"You didn't help a-tall," Penny squawked.

Hanging his head low, Hound Dawg crawled under the creaky porch to whine.

His eyes were just about to shut when, suddenly, his nose began to twitch.

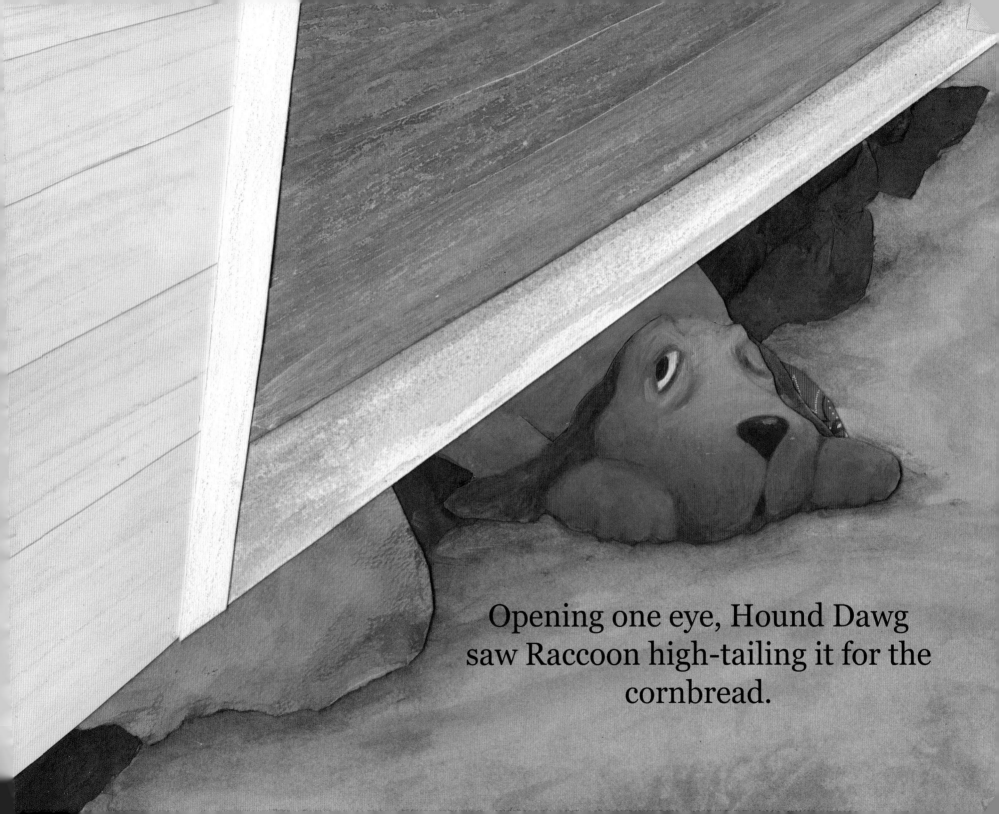

Opening one eye, Hound Dawg
saw Raccoon high-tailing it for the
cornbread.

Bolting from under the porch, he chased the masked bandit deep into the cotton patch, barking and howling all the way.

Hound Dawg came trotting from the cotton patch.
"Look who saved our cornbread," his friends said.

"You earned your share of cornbread," Bessie said, "and a name for yourself, too—Guard Dawg."

"You were purrfect," Calico agreed.
"Eggscellent," Penny nodded.

And from that day 'til this,
Hound Dawg always does—
and gets—his
fair share.

Acknowledgments

I am deeply grateful to Dan Williams, Melinda Esco, Kathy Walton, and Rebecca Allen at TCU Press for their continued support. Sincere appreciation for my SCBWI group, Cynthia Wildridge, Muffet Frische, Nancy Keene, Bill Burton, and Murray Richter. I am grateful to Cynthea Liu and my friend Liz Garton Scanlon for comments and suggestions. Marilyn Z. Joyce, thank you. I'd like to recognize Robert Quackenbush and the late Robert San Souci. Thank you my friends Claude White, Kathy Ritz, Debbie Cox, Jezabel Guadalupe, and Florence Butler, who listened tirelessly. Congratulations to Rebecca Henderson-Smotherman, Linda Whitaker, Aimee Whitaker, Donna Thomas, Sally Keeling, Deborah Taylor, Cynthia Wildridge, Jean Cook, Donna Bartee, and Valerie Bergstrom, cornbread cook-off finalists. Praise for the judges Dick Stenson, Janet Herald, and Regan Vermillion. And cheers to Cheryl Pilgrim, extraordinary illustrator: thank you for bringing Hound Dawg to life. I am especially blessed with my supportive husband, John, who believes in my "Mississippi style of writing."

Facts about Cotton

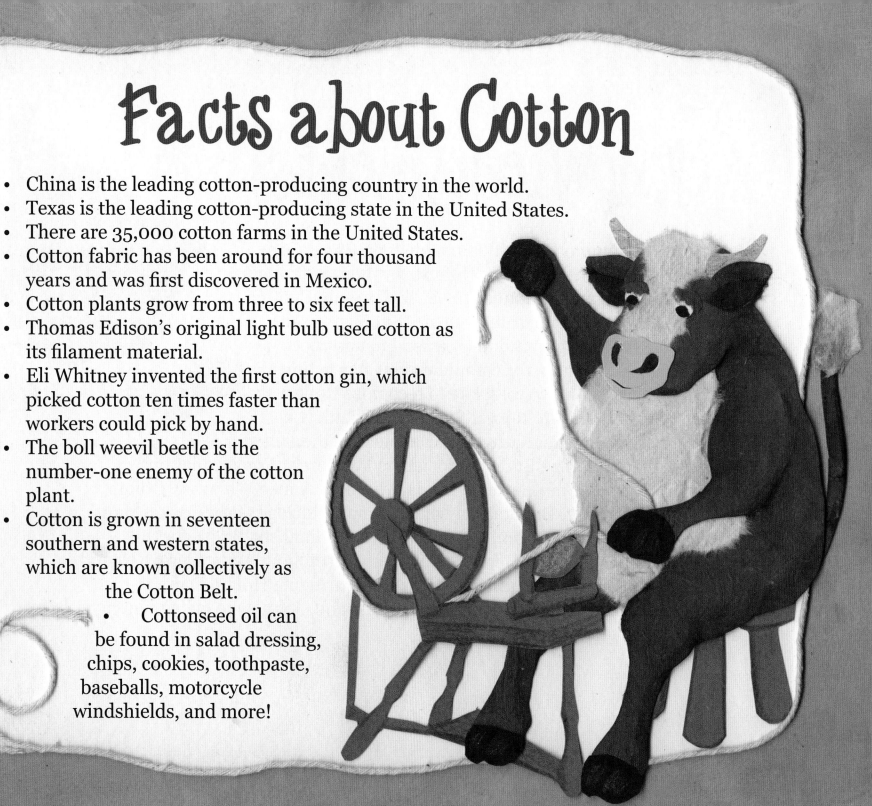

- China is the leading cotton-producing country in the world.
- Texas is the leading cotton-producing state in the United States.
- There are 35,000 cotton farms in the United States.
- Cotton fabric has been around for four thousand years and was first discovered in Mexico.
- Cotton plants grow from three to six feet tall.
- Thomas Edison's original light bulb used cotton as its filament material.
- Eli Whitney invented the first cotton gin, which picked cotton ten times faster than workers could pick by hand.
- The boll weevil beetle is the number-one enemy of the cotton plant.
- Cotton is grown in seventeen southern and western states, which are known collectively as the Cotton Belt.
- Cottonseed oil can be found in salad dressing, chips, cookies, toothpaste, baseballs, motorcycle windshields, and more!

Facts about Corn

- United States is the leading corn-producing country in the world.
- Iowa is the leading corn-producing state in the United States.
- The first corn plants were found in Mexico seven thousand years ago.
- The Spanish name for corn is maíz.
- Corn is planted in spring when soil is warm.
- One plant grows one large and one small ear of corn.
- On most ears of corn, you'll find sixteen rows and eight hundred kernels.
- There is one silk attached to every kernel on a cob. When the silk is pollinated, a kernel forms.
- A corn plant can grow anywhere from five to twelve feet tall.
- Corn can be found in cereals, canned soda, chicken feed, peanut butter, jellies, cake, ice cream, fireworks, crayons, shoe polish . . . you name it.

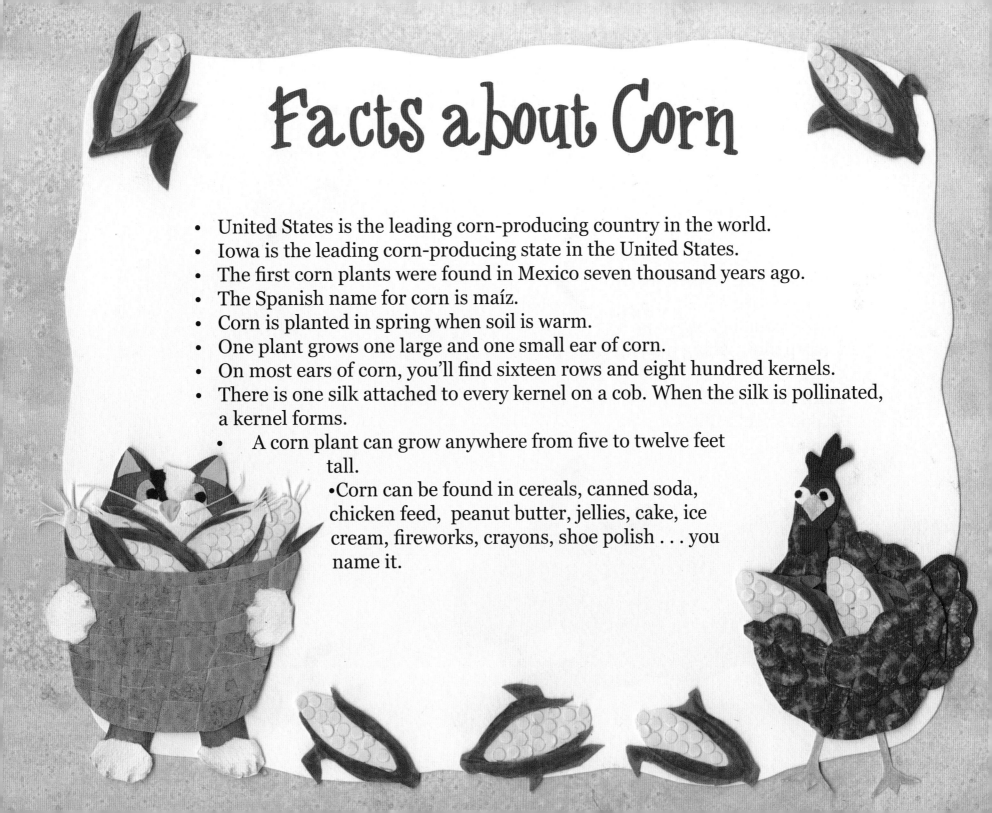

Texas Cornbread

Recipe courtesy of Linda Whitaker of Irving, Texas

Ingredients

1 cup stoneground cornmeal
½ cup all-purpose flour
1 teaspoon salt
¼ teaspoon baking soda
3 teaspoons baking powder
1 egg
1 cup buttermilk
½ cup sweet milk
¼ cup oil

Preheat oven to 450°. Put a 9-inch iron skillet with half of the oil in the oven to heat.

Mix dry ingredients in a large bowl. In a smaller bowl, mix the milks, egg, and the rest of the oil. Mix the wet ingredients into the dry, pour into the iron skillet, and bake 20 minutes. Top should be slightly brown. Cut into pieces when done and put on rack to cool slightly.

Note: To get the crunchy edges, make sure the skillet and oil are very hot before adding the batter. The batter should sizzle when added to the skillet. Immediately return it to the hot oven.

Objectives for Student Learning

- Students will be able to identify the role of the author and illustrator.
- Students will make narrative predictions using the title and illustration on the cover.
- Students will use illustrations throughout to predict what might happen next.
- Students can identify such story elements as beginning, middle, and end, problem and solution.
- Students should share personal experience related to the story (text to self).
- Students will retell the story through drawing or writing.
- Students can respond to story with puppetry, music, or reader's theater.
- Students will be able to identify fiction as made up or fantasy and nonfiction as factual.
- Students can identify the elements of characters, setting, and plot, with support.
- Students should identify important details such as who, what, when, where, and why that relate to the author's purpose.

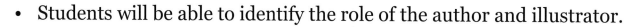

Bibliography

America's Cotton Producers and Importers Cotton Incorporated. Cotton Campus, 2014. Web. 20. July 2014. http://www.cottoncampus.org

McCarty, William H. "Cotton." *World Book Student*. World Book, 2014. Web. 20 July 2014. http://www.worldbookonline.com

Morgan, Dr. Gaylon. Texas A&M University. Kids Education, 2014. Web. 20. July 2014. http://cotton.tamu.edu/KidsEducation.html

National Corn Growers Association. "Corn Education." NCGA Education, 2014. Web. 20 July 2014. http://www.ncga.com/topics/education/education-k-12

National Cotton Council of America. Educational Resources. "Cotton Counts." 2014. Web. 20. July 2014. http://www.cotton.org/pubs/cottoncounts/resources.cfm

Salvador, Ricardo J. "Corn." *World Book Student*. World Book, 2014. Web. 20 July 2014. http://www.worldbookonline.com

Texas Corn Producers. "Corn." Educational Resources. 2014. Web. 20 July 2014. http://texascorn.org/learn-more/educational-resources

Patricia W. Vermillion, librarian at The Lamplighter School in Dallas, is the author of *Texas Chili? Oh My!*, which received a Publication Award in 2015 from the San Antonio Conservation Society.

Cheryl Pilgrim is a writer, illustrator, and former art teacher. She works in a variety of media including pencils, watercolors, oils, acrylics, and collage papers.